Hayley May is a London-based author creating inquisitive stories with a sense of charm for those young readers. Her playful tone draws the audience into the adventures, and the larger-than-life characters at the centre of her entertaining stories. Hayley lives with her husband, two children, and their golden Labrador. When she isn't writing, you will find her running, cooking, or taking long dog walks.

i

WILSON
and
WOODY

Hayley May

AUSTIN MACAULEY PUBLISHERS™
LONDON • CAMBRIDGE • NEW YORK • SHARJAH

A CIP catalogue record for this title is available from the British Library.

ISBN 9781035834860 (Paperback)
ISBN 9781035834877 (Hardback)
ISBN 9781035834884 (ePub e-book)

www.austinmacauley.com

First Published 2024
Austin Macauley Publishers Ltd®
1 Canada Square
Canary Wharf
London
E14 5AA

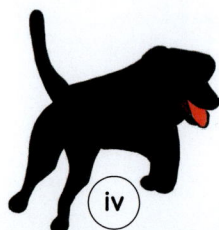

iv

Dedicated to Wilson and Woody, our beloved black Labradors who were taken from us far too soon. Writing about some of their adventures will keep their legacy living on. They really were two very special boys.

Thank you to my husband, Sam, for always being my number one fan. For always encouraging me, believing in me, and pushing me to step out of my comfort zone. I could not have done this without your support and the confidence you have in me.

Thank you to my two beautiful children, who think I am now really cool, for listening endlessly to my storytelling and always giving me very honest feedback.

Thank you, Wilson and Woody, for daily conversations with your tail wags, jumping around, mischievousness and much more. You are missed dearly.

And finally thank you to Austin Macauley for publishing my book. Thank you for all the guidance and support, and for giving me this opportunity.

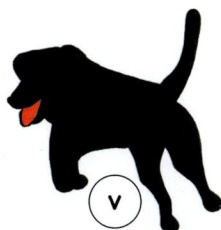

There were once two brothers who loved to talk.
They weren't your ordinary type—four legs, a wagging tail, and a burly bark!
DOGS!
Labradors, to be precise.
Wilson and Woody are what they were called.

This is Wilson

There was once a time that it was just me!
The belly rubs, the treats, the leftovers were all mine. I even got to sleep on the bed sometimes.

Then one day, Mum and Dad brought home an alien!
This alien only had two legs, no tail, no fur BUT a very loud, piercing bark!
It smelled different to me, and I was sure, absolutely sure that it wasn't going to go away!

Beyond the noise, it was quite sweet, and it smiled at me, which made me feel all warm inside, but I really wasn't sure how this was going to work.

Something strange happened right under my nose—Edie, that's what they called her—and I became best friends!
Although Edie was loud, full of energy, and sometimes smelly, she loved me, and I loved her.

She would follow me everywhere, so I followed her everywhere.
The best thing was that she shared her food with me, so when it came to my dinner time, I returned the favour. "No, don't eat that" Mum used to shout. I had told Edie that it was okay, but Mum wanted me to eat it; she was probably worried I wouldn't have enough for myself.

Edie would dress me up; I wasn't that keen, but I let her do it.
I have been superwoman, a vampire, spiderman, and I've worn pink headbands and many stickers!

All this playing around would tire us out, so we'd snuggle on the sofa or on the floor. Occasionally this would result in a little nap.
We were such a great team!

A short time later, my whole world changed again. Another dog!

This one was different to me; it looked a lot like me just a lot smaller.
It followed me everywhere; it ate my food, it stole my bed, it even stole cuddles from me!
Mum, Dad, and Edie loved him.
I'm not sure what they were all thinking—why did we need another dog!
I had Edie, life was great.
They just kept saying "It's okay Wilson, this is your brother."

After what felt like years, however, it was probably only a few days... I realised he, Woody, wasn't so bad, and the fact was he was my brother who was here to stay.
So that was it; we were the three amigos.

Woody grew so quickly, just like Edie did.
Edie would plonk herself on our backs.
I really do think she thought we were horses sometimes.
We played hide and seek, Edie's way.
She would cover us with blankets and then run away laughing.
That laugh was infectious.
I made sure Edie and Woody had the best days.

Early morning walks were so much fun.
Woody and I plunged ourselves into the lake most days.
Mum would yell at us to stop, but we never heard her until it was too late.
She used to say, "Oh you two stink!"

Needless to say, we had to have a bath when we got home.
That wasn't so much fun, but Mum was right that lake did rather stink

But we never learnt.
We jumped into that lake over and over again.

I helped with the gardening; I loved it.
I was so proud at the holes I dug.
I'd end up with a really muddy nose and really muddy paws.
Dad was always shocked at the holes in the garden when he got home
from work. I'm not sure if he was mad or secretly proud.
When the monster machine came out, I tried to be louder than he was...
WOOF WOOF WOOF.

We moved house one day. I'm not one for big changes.
Once I'd sniffed every inch of it, though, I realised our new home was going to be perfect.

The garden was my peaceful place. With birds tweeting, the wind blowing in my ears, I liked to relax out here a lot and sniff the air.

We had been in the new house for a little while, when another alien baby arrived. This one was the loudest of them all.
Baxter, we had another brother.
When was this going to end?
I gave up.

I huffed and puffed and turned those puppy eyes into the eyeball roll!
Yet here I was again.
I couldn't help but love Baxter.
He loved me so much and I loved him.
Baxter grew quickly just like Woody and Edie did. Life just kept getting better and better. We had fun all the time.

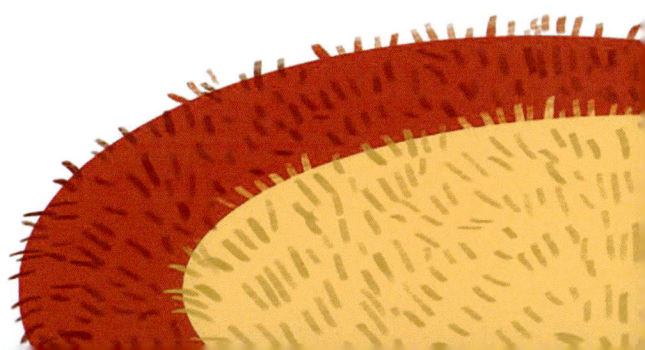

One day we woke up and everything was pure white.
I stood at the door with so many questions flying through my brain.
"Is it safe to go out? Where on earth did it come from? Can I eat it?"
Before I knew it, we were in it. It was cold and crunchy and exhilarating.

That day, we went on a very slippery walk.
Edie and Baxter flew down the cold hill on what looked like uncomfortable beds, and me and Woody followed them, chanting 'woof woof' excitedly.
We couldn't catch them though.

Once we got to the bottom, we would all run back to the top to do it all over again.
In spring, summer, autumn and winter, park life was always the best.
Every day was my favourite day.

"Good boy Will Wills," Mum and Dad would say.
It was then that I knew I was a good boy and doing my job properly.

This is Woody

I'm Woody!
I'm a little younger than Wilson but a little bigger —some say like a panther.
Mum thinks I am exasperating, but really, I am entertaining.

One day Mum moved the bin into the cupboard…
Apparently, when I nosedive into the bin and tip it over, she doesn't like it.
Sometimes I do get stuck, and my back legs and tail just flutter around
in the air until Mum pulls me out.
I don't see the problem.

I pull out the yogurt pots and clean them. I pull out the leftover toast from
breakfast and eat it. Mum hates waste! I even found a piece of chicken
from the Sunday roast. Now that was a treat!

Mum likes a clean house; she's always putting things away.
One day, I thought I'd help as she forgot to put the bread away.
So, I put it away while she wasn't looking. OK I ate the whole thing. Turns out sough dough is R.E.A.L.L.Y good!

Mum, Dad, and the kids go out sometimes, Wilson and I LOVE to play.
We have so much fun running around the house, with cushions flying everywhere, the rug moving and sometimes even the sofa moves too.
Who knew!

But when everyone returns, they don't seem to be too thrilled, and Wilson acts peculiar too. Kind of like.
Squeaky clean!!!

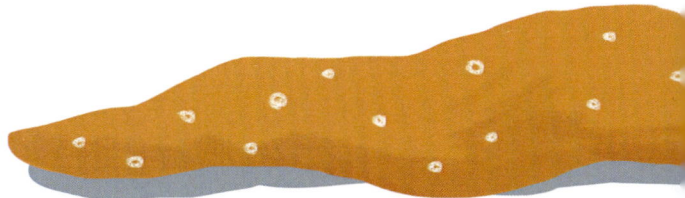

Occasionally, a different human will come to our door.
I always vault over the sofa to shield my family from the stranger.
It's usually a man in a red coat who gives us treats.
Once, he threw the treat at Mum.

I must have worked so well on my ferocious face because he was very startled. I would have just wagged my tail and gone in for a hug if he'd hung around. His loss!

"Do you want to go out?"
We love hearing this; we dance, we bounce, we skip, and even chatter away excitedly every single time so Mum and Dad know we love it. We get to go out into that green space, be free, and meet other people just like us.

The park—I think that's what it's called—it's so wonderful. There are so many different smells; sometimes there is food, but we know to stay away from picnics. The food is always so good, but some of that human type aren't so nice!

We chase the ball; we love this game.
I'm a bit cheeky, though, and when I have the ball, I make Wilson chase me! I'll always give it to him, though, because I love Wilson.

Muddy puddles are the best.
I splash and race through the water.
Sometimes even bathe in it.
It's sooo good until we get home and must have a bath in the garden! We don't laugh too much then!

I love to roll in things; rolling feels so good on my back.
I do get told off for rolling in really smelling stuff though. I think they call this 'fox poo'.

When we get home, we are zonked.
We clamber onto the sofa and sleep.
Sometimes we curl up into a ball, sometimes Wilson is my pillow, and
sometimes we lie on our backs with our legs in the air.
Mum and Dad think this is funny.

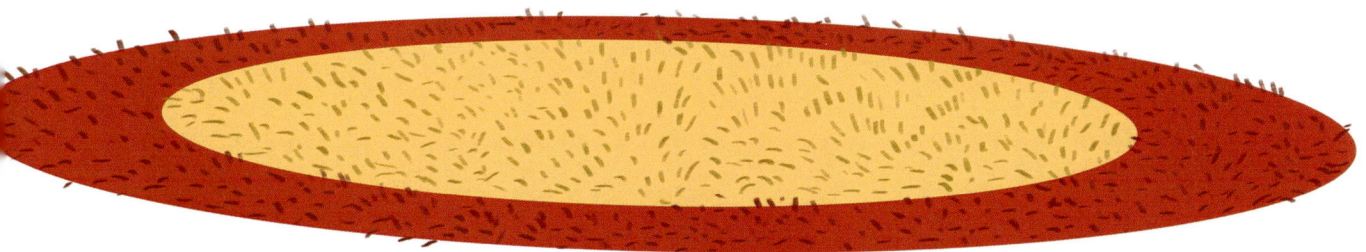

After all the exercise and napping, I'm starving!
I know when it's exactly 5 p.m., so I start to playfully nudge Mum and Dad.
Actually, its usually Dad! He always knows what it is I want.
He can see me wasting away.
I love dinner time.

By the end of the day, I'm so exhausted to move.
I'll snuggle up with Wilson, Mum, Dad and the kids, and I'm content.
I have had a GREAT day.

Mum's forgotten about me being 'playful', or maybe she'd say 'troublesome'.
I drift off to sleep, looking forward to tomorrow.

Just a tale of two dogs.